It's Not About You, Mr. Easter Bunny

A Love Letter About
the True Meaning of Easter

Soraya Diase Coffelt
Illustrated by Tea Seroya

The Love Letters Book Series

NEW YORK

It's Not About You, Mr. Easter Bunny
A Love Letter About the True Meaning of Easter

Published in New York, New York, by Morgan James Publishing. Morgan James and The Entrepreneurial Publisher are trademarks of Morgan James, LLC. www.MorganJamesPublishing.com

The Morgan James Speakers Group can bring authors to your live event. For more information or to book an event visit The Morgan James Speakers Group at www.TheMorganJamesSpeakersGroup.com.

Shelfie

A **free** eBook edition is available with the purchase of this print book.

CLEARLY PRINT YOUR NAME ABOVE IN UPPER CASE

Instructions to claim your free eBook edition:
1. Download the Shelfie app for Android or iOS
2. Write your name in **UPPER CASE** above
3. Use the Shelfie app to submit a photo
4. Download your eBook to any device

ISBN 978-1-68350-063-6 paperback
ISBN 978-1-68350-064-3 eBook
ISBN 978-1-68350-065-0 case laminate
Library of Congress Control Number:
2016907058

In an effort to support local communities, raise awareness and funds, Morgan James Publishing donates a percentage of all book sales for the life of each book to Habitat for Humanity Peninsula and Greater Williamsburg.

Get involved today! Visit
www.MorganJamesBuilds.com

I dedicate this book to my sisters
Sylvia, Martha, Doris and Kathie.

Thanks for all that you have done in
making my life so happy and fulfilled.

God told Abraham that because of his faithfulness, God would bless him and all of his descendants, who would be as numerous as the stars of the sky. **Genesis 15:5; 22:15; Hebrews 11:8-12.**

Children, along with adults, are among Abraham's descendants.

Dear Mr. Easter Bunny

It's Not About You, Mr. Easter Bunny

Dear Mr. Easter Bunny,

I'm a kid who loves bunnies just like you!

You're so-o-o fluffy and cute! I love your long, soft ears, small pink nose, and furry tail. Hopping all around and playing with your friends – what fun you must have all day long!

I know you eat lots of carrots and lettuce. The only question I have is this: "Do your parents make you eat those vegetables?" Mine do! I know vegetables are supposed to be good for me, so that's why I eat them. Is that why you eat them too?

Each year around Easter time, at every store, there are lots of stuffed toy bunnies, chocolate bunnies, fuzzy baby chicks, and baskets full of colorful eggs and candy. One of my favorite parts of the celebration is the egg hunt where my friends and I run around looking for hidden eggs and prizes. We often run so fast in search of the eggs that we topple over each other and fall down laughing.

But Mr. Easter Bunny, I've been wondering how the Easter celebration started. Do you know? Well, I was curious so I asked my teacher about it. She explained it to me and I was really surprised by what she said. I thought you would like to know too.

9

It all began in ancient times (that means a really long time ago). People worshipped all sorts of gods and goddesses (that means they thought they were special and powerful and prayed to them). These people were called pagans. They worshipped a sun god, a rain god, a fire god, and gods or goddesses for each season of the year and for almost everything that existed. Gee … I don't know how they kept track of all those gods and goddesses!

There was a goddess for the spring season and for fertility (that means having lots of babies). She was named Eastre (or Ishtar or Eostre or Ostara, depending on what country you lived in). Doesn't the spelling of her name look familiar?

People even made statues of this goddess and worshipped her. They believed that each year she brought new life. For plants, that meant that they would sprout new green leaves and bloom colorful flowers. For animals, that meant they would have lots of babies.

And that's how bunnies became the center of attention. The ancient Egyptians believed that rabbits were a symbol of fertility because they have lots of babies quickly. They also believed that chicken eggs represented new life because baby chicks are born from eggs.

16

Each spring, the pagans held festivals to celebrate this goddess in hopes that she would bless them. They brought rabbits and colored eggs as gifts for her. They also hung eggs in the temples they had built for her.

As time passed, the beliefs of the ancient Egyptians spread to Europe and then to America. These beliefs grew and expanded as people of different countries and cultures began to celebrate the festival for the goddess Eastre. And that's where you come in! Bunnies were considered special pets of the goddess that could lay colorful eggs. Isn't that funny?! Everyone knows that rabbits don't lay eggs!

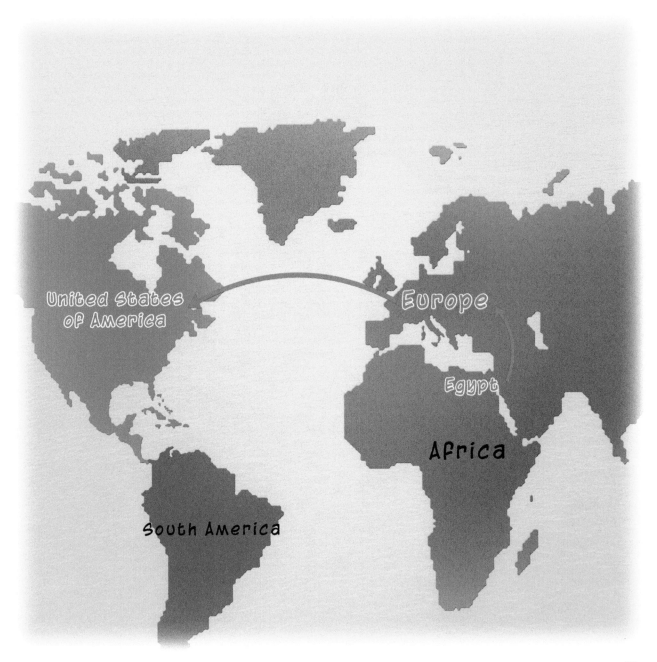

Over the years, the tradition and story have continued to change. No longer is it about a goddess of fertility, but instead it has become all about YOU, the Easter Bunny, who brings gifts to children. So most people only know about the colorful baskets filled with candy and decorated eggs, egg hunts and cute baby chicks, not that it began as a celebration to worship the goddess of spring and fertility. But for a kid like me, it all just seems so-o-o cute and lots of fun.

Well, Mr. Easter Bunny, did you know that Christians also celebrate a very special event each spring? Since I'm a kid, I'm very curious about lots of things. (I think I told you that already.) I wondered whether the Christian celebration had anything to do with the pagan celebration of the goddess Eastre. You probably know that Christians don't worship gods or goddesses. They believe that there is only one true God who created everything in heaven and on earth.

I want to tell you a great big secret, so put your long ears close to my letter. I discovered that the Bible doesn't mention anything about you, Mr. Easter Bunny, or colored eggs, or baby chicks, or egg hunts. The Bible does tell us that God loved us so much that He sent His only Son, Jesus, to save us from sin and death. Jesus died on a cross for us, was buried, and rose from the dead.

For Christians, the resurrection of Jesus represents the beginning of a new spiritual life for each person – sort of a new beginning or a new birth of the person. Each spring, Christians set aside specific days to remember, cherish, and honor what Jesus did for us. Most people call this celebration Easter, but I think it should be called Resurrection Day because it's not about bunnies or spring or a fertility goddess! It's all about Jesus!

So next year when spring comes again, I choose to remember and celebrate what Jesus did for me. I won't forget you, Mr. Easter Bunny, but it's really not about you! However, you can celebrate Jesus too. After all, what's important is not candy (eating too much is not good for our teeth anyway), but the love that God has for all of us because God is love!

Love,
Me

Dear Reader,

Are you a part of God's family? The Bible says that all you have to do is accept God's Son, Jesus, as your Lord and Savior. If you want to celebrate Jesus and make Him Lord of your life, say this simple prayer:

"Dear Lord Jesus, thank you for loving me so much that You died on the cross for my sins. I ask you to be my Lord and Savior.

Amen."

About the Author

Soraya Diase Coffelt is a lawyer and former judge as well as the mother of two sons. She has volunteered and served as a lay children's minister for many years. God has given her many creative ideas for ministering His Word to children, and her books are among them.

In 2012, she established a non-profit foundation, As the Stars of the Sky Foundation, Inc., to assist with the physical and spiritual needs of children. All proceeds from the sale of her books go toward the Foundation.

If you have enjoyed this book and want to learn more about Jesus' life, I invite you to purchase a copy of another book in The Love Letters series:

It's Not About You, Mr. Santa Claus
It's Not About You, Mrs. Turkey
It's Not About You, Mr. Pumpkin
And more....

To order your copy, please go to:
www.asthestarsofthesky.org
or email us: info@asthestarsofthesky.org

CPSIA information can be obtained
at www.ICGtesting.com
Printed in the USA
LVOW05*1439170217

524629LV00025B/317/P

9 781683 500650